The Life and Poetry of
of
Ralph Harry Nesson

Please direct inquiries to Chava Boyett: chavaboyett@gmail.com

Cover photo: Ralph and daughter Chava by Bob Nesson

Interior photos from family archives

Photo of Ralph singing courtesy of Kirk Lanier Photography

ISBN: 978-0-578-89099-9

Library of Congress Control Number: 2021907418

Contents

Introduction

The Life of Ralph Harry Nesson

In October 2001 the *Arkansas Democrat-Gazette* published an interview in its Northwest Arkansas section titled "Ralph Harry Nesson: Lifelong Education." Among other questions that focused primarily on his philanthropic work, he was asked about one life goal he hadn't yet achieved. His answer was "self-publishing a book of poetry." Well, Ralph, it took a little digging, but now you finally have.

Ralph Nesson was born February 27, 1947 in Norwood, Massachusetts. He was raised in a tree-lined neighborhood in Brookline, a close-in Boston suburb, among mostly Jewish neighbors, many of them immigrants or children of immigrants from Eastern Europe who'd escaped the Soviet pogroms or the Nazi Holocaust. He lived with his mother, Freda, and father, William, his older sister, Carol, and brother, Bob, in one crowded floor of a two-family home. Upstairs were his aunt, uncle and cousins, including his first cousin, Peter Blumenthal, with whom Ralph shared a lifelong deep friendship. For Ralph's entire childhood, his father Bill worked six and seven days a week in a family-owned retail business, Nesson's Department

Store. His work ethic provided for the family and allowed Ralph and his siblings to go to summer camp each year. That experience shaped Ralph's love of the outdoors. He and his brother Bob went on many hiking, camping and climbing expeditions together over the years. They always greeted each other with the same affectionate nickname. "Hey, Ness!" they'd say, laughing and smiling when they saw one another or spoke over the phone.

He attended public schools in Brookline and earned his undergraduate degree in American history at Hobart College in Geneva, New York. After college in 1968, he joined the Volunteers In Service to America program (VISTA), a domestic Peace Corps. He was assigned to work at a mental health rehabilitation center on Chicago's north side. There he met VISTA volunteer and future wife, Kathleen "Kate" Conway. Both were part of the era's counterculture, wearing their hair long and approaching their careers and lives with optimism, idealism and liberal viewpoints. Coincidentally, Kate had grown up just twenty-five miles away from Ralph in Beverly, Massachusetts. The Vietnam war was raging, as was the anti-war movement. For their first date they went to a concert headlined by the singer Joni Mitchell. Soon they moved to San Francisco, where their first child was born. When their daughter, Chava, was nearing age one, Ralph and Kate relocated across the country, settling in Arkansas in 1974. There they had two sons, Liam in 1976, and Ben in 1980.

After moving to Fayetteville and earning his master's degree in education from the University of Arkansas, Ralph began his career writing grants and planning outreach programs as a Community Development Specialist for the Economic Opportunity Agency (EOA) of Washington County. In search of new and creative ways to combat poverty, he observed, "It just became very obvious to me over time that women and children are among the largest group of poor people in our community and in the larger society." Ralph's steady and insightful leadership style propelled him to the position of EOA director in 1985.

Ralph focused on innovative ways to tackle economic and educational disparity. In 1984, he and Marjorie Wolf co-founded a scholarship program for low-income single parents serving two counties in Northwest Arkansas, Ralph taking Washington County and Marjorie, Benton County. Their keen awareness of the needs of others hit the mark and the programs were immediately successful. They took their efforts a bold step forward and decided to replicate the model across the state. Thus, the Arkansas Single Parent Scholarship Fund (ASPSF) was born, with Ralph serving as Executive Director.

Ralph had a talent for cultivating support through donor relationships and effective fundraising. Hillary Clinton, then First Lady of Arkansas, served as ASPSF Board President for the first three years, resigning when she and Bill Clinton moved to the White House.

As Executive Director of ASPSF, Ralph raised tens of millions of dollars for the organization over the next twenty-three years. He secured endowment funds from notable community leaders such as Bernice Jones and organizations such as the Tyson Foundation and the Willard and Pat

Walker Foundation. Although he was adept at building strong relationships with influential philanthropists, Ralph's personal affect was unassuming and down-to-earth. He was reliably frugal, always driving economy cars or a beat-up pickup truck and drawing a modest salary. He was most comfortable in a tee-shirt and shorts, only wearing a suit and tie when the occasion required that he do so. Always drawn to the quirky and offbeat, he preferred yard sales and thrift shops to department stores, and independently owned diners to chain restaurants.

Ralph said, "Offering scholarships to people, encouraging them to go pursue their education . . . helps people to unlock their own potential in ways they otherwise might not be aware of. That's inspiring to me." A recent study shows that ASPSF recipients have a 92 percent retention and graduation rate, and a 90 percent employment rate at above poverty-level. "Think about it," Ralph wrote. "For every single mother or father we assist to succeed, there are more and more children who are learning the true value of education at their parents' knees. One person's success then becomes five, then ten, then twenty and on and on." Ralph directly and indirectly helped thousands of people to become more educated, empowered and self-determining.

According to Tyler Clark, Executive Director of Single Parent Scholarship Fund of Northwest Arkansas, one of the original two programs and an affiliate of ASPSF, the Northwest Arkansas chapter of the organization has awarded scholarships to approximately 10,000 recipients in a total amount of $6.9 million as of 2020. This placed money in the hands of impoverished single parents as they worked to complete career-focused college degrees or skills trade certifications.

According to Ruthanne Hill, Executive Director of the statewide Arkansas Single Parent Scholarship Fund (ASPSF), since its inception the organization has awarded a total of 51,242 scholarships in the dollar value of $31,758,127 state-wide as of February 2021.

"Ralph and Marjorie were onto something so beautifully simple and yet so crucial to moving families out of poverty," says Hill. "If you help people financially, while affording them dignity and respect and encouraging them along the way, they can and will do the work to undertake difficult life-changes, altering the path of their families for generations to come."

Ralph was also an active Northwest Arkansas Rotary Club member, often appealing to membership for various fund-raising efforts. Ralph would not hold back on those efforts. He took the annual "Polar Bear Plunge" into ice-cold water to raise money for the Special Olympics. One year he showed up at Rotary Club dressed in his swim trunks, snorkel, mask and fins with two ladies dressed as mermaids, one on each arm, to grab attention for the cause. Needless to say, he was the top fund-raiser for that year's Polar Bear Plunge!

Ralph's pursuits outside of his professional life included speaking Spanish, reading, traveling, gardening, sailing, listening to jazz, storytelling, scrabble playing and Major League baseball fandom. He never lost sight of his Boston roots—he was a passionate Red Sox fan. On September 28, 1960, when he was thirteen years old, he skipped school with his best friend, Jimmy Wallen, to go to Fenway Park to see the historic last game of his hero Ted Williams. In the eighth inning, Williams hit a grand slam home run, now immortalized in a famous essay by John Updike ("Hub Fans Bid Kid Adieu," published in the October 22, 1960 issue of the *New Yorker*).

As an active and dedicated congregation member of Temple Shalom in Fayetteville, Ralph regularly attending Friday Sabbath services, celebrating Jewish holidays and often leading informal ceremonies in small, family-focused gatherings. He loved to make potato latkes and coconut macaroons. Ralph played an instrumental role in fundraising for the Temple Shalom construction in its current modern building on Sang Avenue. Ralph and the temple president, Bill Feldman, befriended local developer Fadil Bayyari, who is a Palestinian Muslim. This resulted in Bayyari's contracting company completing the build of the Temple at cost. This unusual alliance was significant enough to become the focus of a 2007 *New York Times* article.

Ralph loved taking his children and nephews to baseball games at Fenway Park. He also loved to travel the globe. He traveled with his wife to Spain, France, Ireland, Israel, South Korea and New Zealand. He and Kate rented an apartment in coastal Carboneras, Spain in 2003. That led to his interest in the Camino de Santiago pilgrimage trail in Spain. In the summer of 2004 he hiked the trail from Leon to Santiago de Compostela (a 152-mile distance), a portion of it with his dear friend Ray Somera. Ray and his wife Maryanne then completed the entire 500-mile length of the trail the following year.

Ralph found great joy in being a father and grandfather. He had three children with Kate: Chava Nesson Boyett, Liam Conway-Nesson, and Benerin Conway-Nesson. He enjoyed loving and close relationships with his grandsons Tate Boyett and Jett Boyett in Fayetteville, Arkansas, and his granddaughters Chloe Nesson and Eleanor Nesson in Hawaii. He and Kate visited Hawaii annually to spend time with them.

Ralph retired with a bang at the Ralph-a-Palooza Roast & Toast held at the Fayetteville Town Center on February 28, 2013. The event raised some $60,000 for the ASPSF and marked the end of his 23 years as Executive Director with the organization.

Post-retirement, Ralph couldn't stop fundraising for good causes. He acted on this passion by starting the non-profit Northwest Arkansas Books for Kids to promote literacy for underserved children in public schools. He did an annual fundraiser walk, a 100-mile trek from Fayetteville, through Farmington, Prairie Grove, Lincoln and Siloam Springs—and then back—to raise awareness for the importance of early reading. In his view, "Pure family literacy is what this is all about. Encouraging parents to read with their children from infancy onward to keep lots of books in the home, to enrich the family atmosphere with creative activities, helping children to develop their minds so when they are starting school they are on equal footing with all the other children who have possibly more advantages."

On December 31, 2019, just one week prior to his passing, Ralph posted this last message on his Facebook page: "Happy and Healthy New Year everyone! Let's make 2020 a year of peace throughout the world, progress in helping each other thrive, and unity in seeing every person as a brother and sister deserving of respect and understanding. We are all in this together!!!"

On Friday, January 3, 2020, Ralph went on a bike ride with his five-year-old grandson, Jett, to Gregory Park in Fayetteville, Arkansas. While attempting to traverse a raised bike ramp, he suffered a terrible fall from his bike, which resulted in a severely damaged spinal cord, an injury that proved unrecoverable. His family made the difficult decision to remove him from life support on Monday, January 6, 2020. Ralph was seventy-two years old, just one month shy of his seventy-third birthday. Hillary Clinton sent Ralph's family a personal condolence letter and published this message online: "I'm sending my condolences to all mourning the passing of Ralph Nesson. Ralph was a passionate advocate for families; we started the Arkansas Single Parent Scholarship Fund together in 1990, which has awarded 40,000 scholarships to single parents. May his memory be a blessing."

TRIBUTES

Bob Nesson, brother

I'd like to start with a quote, written by Jamie Anderson, that seems appropriate: "Grief, I've learned, is really just love. It's all the love you want to give, but cannot. All of that unspent love you want to give, but cannot. All that unspent love gathers in the corners of your eyes, the lump in your throat, and in the hollow part of your chest. Grief is just love with no place to go."

Ralph Nesson was my little brother, and it makes no sense that he should pre-decease me. I think of Ralph every day, and cry repeatedly when I can't talk with him as we so often did. Many of those talks took place by phone, but were best when we were together having a brother-to-brother adventure: paddling down the beautiful Buffalo River in Arkansas, or climbing mountains in New Hampshire and other states.

We had much in common, but the meaning and intent of his poetry was somewhat *elusive* to me—to the point where I barely read it over the many years. Ralph stopped sending his poetry to me when it was clear to him that I "didn't get it" and when we had pressing life issues to deal with. Reading his words now, after he's gone, reveals how prescient and deeply realistic and sensitive his thinking was. Now I get it.

His gift to all of us is this legacy of important thoughts, shaped into the beautiful poetry that a reader can share. Along with his children Chava, Liam and Ben, his beloved wife Kate, and grandchildren and others in Ralph's family, I hope that these prefaces will frame Ralph's collected verse in ways that contextualize his life experiences in the years we were all so fortunate to share with him. In some ways, his words transform the grief we feel, and give us a place to go.

Chava Nesson Boyett, daughter

I think about who my father was and what he offered to the world and I am overwhelmed with tender gratitude for his kind heart and generous nature. There are so many things for which a person is remembered, maybe stories about what they said or did or awards won and works published. But I think most of all, it is the emotional connection, the vibration or energy of their spirit that we most strongly recall.

My dad's energy was gentle kindness, a comforting presence and playfulness. It was also in his nature to help people who were in distress. The many single moms who received the scholarships for which Ralph raised funds, the son of a friend who was having mental illness issues, the little girl next-door who was neglected by her parents, the old cat he just couldn't put down. And the very first time I saw my dad cry, when he learned of John Lennon's tragic death in winter of 1980.

My dad had a rich interior life. He felt and thought about things deeply. As you will realize from his poetry, he certainly contemplated death in many different contexts. I know he considered the human circumstance of mortality quite often and on some level had come to terms with it. Although his own death was sudden and unpredictable, I do not believe Ralph had a great fear of death. I believe he had processed this inevitability through his grief over losses of dear friends and family as well as through his beloved literature, and likely through writing the poetry you will read here. His only dread seemed to be the possibility of losing his mental function and becoming someone who needed to be cared for. Any brief conversations we had about those possibilities brought a shade of concern and sadness to his eyes. Most of the time, he was robust and full of energy and took pleasure and enjoyment from life. He had seen deterioration of loved ones and that possible future depressed him. The way he died, swiftly, at a relatively "young" old age, while still active and healthy up until the last few days, seemed to suit his sensibilities. Few of us get to choose the circumstances of our exit but I do believe he would have chosen this way over any alternatives that may have included languishing in a deteriorating state.

I fear that the onset of years may dull my memories of my dad and I very much want to cherish and preserve the spirit of his heart in his words for myself and my descendants. I want to petrify his words in amber so we can turn them over and over in our warm hands for years to come. Few are lucky enough to have their loved one's deepest thoughts expressed and articulated in beautiful language recorded and preserved. It is such a gift that he left us with his words, his heart and mind bled onto the page. To commune with him in this way by reading his thoughts expressed as lovely words is a rare privilege. I want to share his kind heart with the world.

Liam Conway-Nesson, son

Why didn't Dad attempt to publish his poetry? Beyond the few dedications printed for tributes or memoriam events, I don't think he tried to gain a wider audience. He actually created an extensive tome of poetry, stories and spoken children's tales—and jokingly imagined himself a wandering storyteller. Was it humility, lack of time, or lack of confidence that kept him from this attempt at publication? Perhaps it was busy-ness, a seeming tirelessness for lending a hand to others.

He also didn't get to seriously collecting his work, probably because he was always doing the extraordinary for family, friends, acquaintances and often strangers. Whether flying to Seattle to help Cousin Martin find a senior care facility; helping nurse his sister Carol in her recovery from a car accident; sitting at our friend Phyllis's bedside while she was in a coma; offering to cover a motel room for a down-on-his-luck transient; or, bolstering a son with encouragement on a frequent call home to Pop, Ralph cared for those close to him.

What concerned my father was being there for people who asked for help. He genuinely wanted to make a positive difference in people's lives. For so many, he found a way to do that. His career was plainly and creatively focused on this incessant search to improve the underdog's stead. Yet, at times he neglected his closest relationships while still on this altruist's pursuit. He was both careful and carefree in his affections; he even loved carelessly and made mistakes that caused himself and others heartache. His was a charmed life, with a wide gamut of joy-filled, painful and exquisite remembrances. To these reflections on his life, I now have to bend to the empty space, the dull ache that reminds me that I won't see or talk with him again.

And then I remind myself to focus on the living—as he would point out. His three children, and four grandchildren, are embodiments of his desire to affect the world positively. He would often encourage us to do good works, to carry a helping hand onward. But who could achieve feats of selflessness as he had? He is a tough act to follow—it can't be done. And yet, it doesn't have to be. Parts of him are here, with me, my siblings, his grandchildren—and all those who feel his absence.

With this mix of love, admiration and recognition of his fallibility, I knew my Dad as a romantic, a sentimental soul who thought intently about his place among us. Mystery, truth, butterflies, how we come into and leave this existence—these were all easy conversation topics between father and son. I clearly remember conversations over and through these ideas with him. What a gift, to be able to speak with and know my Dad in this way.

Rather than getting serious about publishing his written work, Dad wanted his living relationships and living work to show us what he felt deepest. One of his many pursuits was poetry—and so, what follows is a loose collection of verse, found in his ragtag files, handed from his wife to their daughter and, with bittersweet effort, pieced together shortly after he passed. They are earnest, honest pieces that speak to the magic and miracle he saw in life, which we are fortunate to have shared with him.

Ben Conway-Nesson, son

My Dad Lives in a Lighthouse
a poetic tribute

My dad lives in a lighthouse. I go there every year to help him change the Light. Once I arrive in midafternoon, he usually has my cot and Mexican blanket ready in the corner.

My father loves to get up early and stare at the stars. This makes the evening a short one. Most times we have a bowl of soup for supper. We like to reminisce about old times, then go to bed.

As a small child he would tell me that you don't have to have nightmares, you can control your dreams. And since that time, we enjoyed talking about the flights we would take in our subconscious. They would be unparalleled treks across open seas, vast deserts and gorgeous mountain ranges.

Then as if hurled out of a cannon my dad would be on the deck overlooking the ocean and gazing up at the stars. I would gingerly follow him out there, as if not wanting to disturb the gods.

On the deck he would locate all the constellations, detail the conditions of the sea, then describe the wind. But this time was different, I had to tell him I wouldn't be coming anymore. With only the foresight a father could have, he told me "I know son."

As the stars started to disappear we hugged and told each other that our love was so deep, it would always be felt from there on that deck overlooking the sunrise to eternity.

SELF

Miracles

I believe in miracles
Don't know what causes them
but after all, they surround me like a thousand butterflies in
flight

I believe in God
Don't know what s/he is
Or even if it makes sense to believe
so I just trust
that whatever caused it all
is off somewhere making butterflies

Oh I do trust
Who wouldn't? Given the miracle of each morning!
Of each breath
Of each evening when the sun turns flaming orange and
disappears

Let's just say it is a mystery of miracles
Caused by I don't know what . . . but call it God
and I'm glad to be filled with wonder
as the butterflies flutter by

At Work on My Memoirs

There is the faint hum of something live
Off the kitchen
In the dark
Where the spiders are at their elaborate work
In dirt-filled corners and lightly descending dust.

There is the faint hint of something unresolved,
Over near the photographs by the mantel
Emanating from the bookshelves
Where the past 52 years hissing and sparking,
Like a short-circuited life.

The mystery of unfulfilled dreaming,
Plans still on the drawing board,
Corners brown and curling, hard to decipher,
The years required to make things heavy and forgotten.

And from the bedroom,
Yearning deep and throaty,
Hoarse with whispers still pouring out
With all their need unveiled.

I sit at the writing table,

Not a word yet down,
The clock ticking softly,
Hands moving forward,
All the time in the world.

I Knew It Would Happen Like This

I knew it would happen like this,
One day I'd come a thousand miles or more
and find no home to come back to,
the sisters: my mother, my aunt
grown too old to wait for me,
helped into apartments empty of history,
where one's arms hang limp
and mind grows dim,
furniture given to grandchildren to whom
the old chairs and beds mean nothing,
just something temporary
until they can afford better.

I knew it would come to this
I'd walk down the canopied street
bathed in maple leaves and shadows
and find them both removed,
unfamiliar cars in driveway,
new curtains in windows,
a strange chair on porch.
I'd linger by the front stairs
where my cousin Peter and I

played an improvised game
with a tennis ball and were chased away
for making too much noise

I would visit the places arranged for them
and feel sorry only for myself,
watching them shuffle, bent over, from room to tiny room
offering me footstools and afghans and framed pictures
all to keep unburdening for the journey ahead,
and add to mine, grappling with how they belonged to me
and I to them,
until like the house now empty of us all,
they soon would be gone and I, some day, too

Gifts

To fuse into acts of kindness,
I accept the gifts placed before me
like pirate gold,
a thousand dollars here or there
in crisp new bills,
handed over, placed before me
like spoils of a game of chance,
no names attached,
the anonymity requested,
a shadow on a wall.

Put it to some good use
whispers a voice
no mention where it came from,
but if you must,
a friend whose name is lost.

Conscience is a wrestler,
denial of whence the riches came,
imagining it will not ever matter,
that I can live with all the gifts
bestowed like this, received

as might a beggar,
his cup out in the rain.

In a theater of the wordless,
envelopes delivered in pantomime,
the moment past when I, the only player,
can see beyond stage and curtain,
am left to bear the weight
of what has come out of the dark.

Truth, You Old Dog

I am searching for you
in the naked wilderness of *what passes* for my life,
whose sorrows and hidden mysteries
are secreted among my dreams,

I am keeping an eye out for you
on the rooftops and deep in the cellars of thought,
in cold addictive places,
around sharp corners and cul de sacs.
on the tip of my tongue,
at the end of my manhood,
through whatever seeps in through my ears,
and floats there, supine and vulnerable.

In your many disguises
you have loosened my grip,
taunted me by remaining at arm's length,
as one would tease a dog and make it jump
for something beyond its reach.

Frothing at the mouth, begging, pleading,
I am panicked with a need for you,
bent and pulled and ruined on the rack of confusion,

all the while nipping at my own heels
as your pure, unsullied hymenic membrane
floats beyond, content within yourself, singing your own
hymns,
virginal and holy, blessed and christened,
waving aloft like the banner of a beatified saint,
unreachable,
    untouchable,
        immune
You are so damn hard to get hold of,
a conjurer standing before me,
performing trick after trick with unrelenting speed,
you are as impossible
as a miracle
and as common as two hands.

In Which I Lose My Grip

They chose me for the mental health award,
a chance to hang another plaque upon the wall,
to put my face in the paper,
alongside the mayor's and photos of the Girl Scouts.
They wanted to stuff me full of food at a banquet,
pat me on the back, recognize me for all of my efforts
to keep other people sane,
before sending me out to do some more good.

But my wife wouldn't agree to it,
she said you are too crazy this year,
you've had enough of backslapping
and dressing up and putting a noose around your neck.
Give it a rest and maybe they'll invite you back the next time
they run out of martyrs.

So now I can only dream of what it would be like
to be Mr. Mental Health and have a big grin on my face
and represent the perfect specimen of mind and matter,
to give speeches to the Chamber of Commerce
and be a good example to the youth of today.

"My fellow bathers in the pub waters of clear thinking,
keep your minds free of panic and fear,
allow yourselves not a thought in gray or black
but always strive to walk
the straight and narrow path of upright living,
the *only* one worth taking.
Approach each day with the certainty that one healthy
thought
is worth another and another.
And keep a good supply of them,
keep a whole basement full of them,
rent a self-storage unit and stock it to the ceiling with them,
for you can never have enough.
Do not give into doubt,
put those questions aside, concentrate on the tried and true,
for the path of plumbing the depths can only lead you
downward.
Have faith, fellow positive thinkers, it's a whole lot easier
to move straight ahead than veer off course."

Oh, I wish I had been able to give that speech,
that my depression and suicidal thoughts
had lightened up for just an hour or two

Tolstoy's Grandmother

After failing all of my sanity tests
And leaving the Ten Commandments behind for good,
I borrowed a dollar for the price of admission
To the state hospital charity ward,
And began my studies in earnest.

Someone had left a book about Tolstoy in the toilet stall,
An enigmatic inscription on the inside cover,
A drawing of a sleeping woman
And the words "See page 203 for details"

And turning to that page, I learned that Leo's grandmother
Had difficulty sleeping, so much in fact that she hired a blind storyteller
To weave her dreams of giants and dragons with five heads
Bringing her treasures and asking for her hand

When the bitter cold of the Russian winter made her shiver,
She'd invite Leo under the covers
Where he'd listen raptly to the stories floating over the bed,
Loosed from the blind man's mouth like long, slow grace notes

Bending and handing and turning, choreographed like a
ballerina's shoes

It was the grace notes that brought on her dreams,
Lifting, wafting, soaring high above the bed with her
grandson
Tucked snugly in the V of her knees, between the soft pillows
of her breasts.
It was the grace notes undulating through her in a melancholy
way,
Sewn and quilted and woven together sublimely,
Passionate waves of notes, floating in on her shores,
The giants and dragons elongating like snakes, like long
ribbons
Wrapping and flowing and tying around her,
Poor Leo almost drowning, suffocating underneath her
As she rolled, as she moaned, and enveloped him . . .

The servants, at this point, would lead the blind man out of
the room,
The story slowly diffusing,
The heated notes dropping down from the crescendoed
heights and falling,
The calm returning,
The snores of the grandmother echoing off the lacquered
ceiling
Like distant thunder,

The silence of the early morning eerie like an empty pond.

Awakening, Leo's grandmother would shake him and
Ask what happened at the end of the story
And he would have an answer for her,
Always an answer as good as the storyteller could have told it,
Of the dragon with five heads kissing her, one set of lips after
another,
Until the fifth transformed into a handsome prince
Who slew his four brothers with one swipe of his blade,
Lifted her onto his stallion,
And rode off across the frozen steppes
To his castle in the golden dawn.

At the end of that page,
Someone suggested in the margin
To refer to another chapter of the book,
But there was someone knocking on the toilet stall door
And I had to leave Tolstoy's life
For the next patient.

Hitler and Me Listening to Miles

We were sitting there together,
Elbows almost touching,
Slowly rhythmically moving our heads,
As Miles wailed up on the stage, all blues, all blues,
His eyes penetrating the audience
Lips curled dark and puffed against his horn.

We were sitting side by side,
Swaying our knees, flowing, grooving
With the solo on *So What*,
Feeling what Miles was feeling
Floating away on the high notes,
Balancing our souls on the low,
Sipping wine and tapping our fingers,
Locked in a duet of feeling
Only Miles' people can know,
Only those who truly dig Miles can feel.

When the question slipped out
Like the very next note from the holy trumpet itself,
WHY?
And he shifted in his seat and looked at me,
His eyes red with pain,

His jaw taut with the wrenching loss,
His nose glistening with tears cascading down
And said I never heard music like this,
I never let it in,
I didn't know what it could do to me.

And he turned back to the stage,
And let it in again,
Let it do what it could to him

And six million Jews and two million Gypsies
And seventeen million Russians
And three million children
Climbed out of their graves
And thanked Miles for letting in the light.

The Path to Shalom

The path to shalom is courage
To awaken with the hope of orphans,
To drink from the cup of one
Who has raised his hand against you,
To pray in his language, with his words,
To sow seed in the trusting earth,
To risk everything that is sacred to you
And dream under the same healing moon.

The path to shalom is imminent,
Yet littered with bleeding wings,
With bones and memories,
With unnoticed light.

The path to shalom divides and consumes us
With warnings, with awful deeds,
Pitting brother against brother,
Exposing and forsaking us,
Like lambs to the sacrifice,
Shivering on the altar.

We cling to it, this path,
With the staying power of angels,

Embracing friends who were enemies,
The disillusioned, the misguided,
And those who fall from grace, waving false Torahs,
Claiming theirs as the one true gift.

The path to shalom is never abandoned,
Though despair like a threatened snake
Rattles its warnings,
Though bones and memories find us weeping,
Though our children must bury us
And complete our tasks

The path to shalom is courage,
The courage to awaken with orphaned hope,
To drink from the cup of one
Who has raised his hand against you,
Pray with the same gentle words,
Risk everything held sacred,
And dream under the same healing moon.

Storyteller

I am telling a creation story,
Animals discovering the firmament under water,
Clouds circling over the voice of God.

The schoolchildren at my feet
Are suddenly Shoshones,
Enraptured by a silent campfire,
Eyes glazed by inner visions,
Of a world being born.

FAMILY

For Mother

Your journey ends,
eyelids fluttering closed,
lips motionless from last calm breath,
fingers lightly perched on throat,
as if adjusting a necklace,
one arm over womb,
moist hair splayed across pillow,
youthful cheeks soft and furred and drawn,
nose glistening,
the nose you said I inherited,
face so still,
so momentarily, eternally still,
while through the summer air,
sweetened by honeysuckle and mint,
the muted clatter of newlywed cans
tied to a bumper is heard,
a honeymoon begun,
a spirit flown.

A year to the day you traveled here with me,
the South so exotic,
bucolic was the word you chose
for pasturing cows out your front window,

a pond with honking geese across the road,
gentle Ozarks horizon hinted in the distance.

Sitting on your porch,
clematis and morning glory vines,
and hollyhock about to bloom,
you smile,
that twinkling amused Fredi smile,
and look at me and say,
"It's not Brookline!"

I have a vision of you
just two weeks past,
gamely climbing down a rock-strewn embankment,
crimson life-jacket dwarfing your shoulders,
daintily poised in bow of canoe,
lifting a long wooden paddle,
pulling it through Beaver Lake water
in steady strokes,
transforming yourself
into the athletic teenager of your stories,
once again graceful and lithe,
traversing the grass tennis courts of 1920's Franklin Field,
crawl stroking in the Gloucester surf,
making plans for picnics and movies and dances at
Norumbega dusk,
so full of life, so full of life.

My reverie is disturbed by keening and weeping,
tears surround me,
my lips are on your cheek,
Your younger sister grasps your hand,
your oldest child's ear is suddenly on your unmoving chest,
deep sobs welling up inside him,
your daughter has turned her eyes upward,
as if to guide your soul ascending.
Mourning doves coo,
mocking birds click their summer song,
the room becomes silent of voices,
the hearts of your grandchildren beat with wonder,
with pain,
feeling you leaving them behind.

My Father's Cage

The store allowed him out at seven,
The privilege of a doomed captive
Forever submerged in 1952,
Though he lived another seventeen years.

Pants without style and plastic penholder in dress shirt,
His collapsed brother Louis had left him the rusted crank
With which to raise the awnings every night,
Before steering home down Route One
And over the Tobin Bridge,
Where for twenty seconds he could steal glances at the harbor
And perhaps sight a ship headed out to sea.

We would absently watch him at dinner,
Our stomachs tired from waiting, openly hostile to the idea of
him,
A father lost within his business,
Old and forgotten in his prime,
A specter of what not to become.

Oblivious to the electricity of children,
He would be snoring on the living room chair,
Newspaper on lap,

Cigarette cold and harmless,
A thin vulnerable throat bathed in lamplight.

I awoke to the smell of coffee,
The dull squeal of a transmission in reverse,
The receding thrum of tires on asphalt,
As he moved back on to the treadmill.

In My Grandfather's House

I wandered through the old house
and into the silent attic,
where an old book lay open by a window,
soft with the work of spiders.
I took the book in my lap,
turning the fragile pages slowly,
reading of a small boy who is lost in a forest,
so lost that he knows only to listen to the wind
and let it guide him to a cottage small and forlorn,
hidden in a glen.

the cottage is that of a thin hermit, wise and kindly
and the book in the attic tells of the hermit singing to the boy,
filling his ears with mysteries,
of the days when the wee and gentle people
lived under the leaves of trees
in turtle shells abandoned,
and often slept in the nests of robins,
keeping warm their eggs.
But a great storm came one night
and blew about the shells and nests and leaves where rested
the wee people,

scattering them far and wide about the forest,
causing them to be sad and lonely and to miss each other's
merriment.

Only the smallest of the wee people knew the trick
of speaking with the robins and one of them listened to his
pleas,
then called to the others for help.
The birds began to sweep low and high with their wings,
finding the wee people and lifting them in their beaks,
bringing them all together again
from whence the wind had blown them.
They were joyous and sang and danced all around,
until the full moon brought sleep to their eyes,
when they slept in peace within the nests of the robins.

The lilt of the hermit's voice
lulled the boy into a sleep of his own,
deep into a reverie of wee people carrying him out of the
hermit's cottage
and into a glade gleaming with sunlight
where his mother and sister were twining dandelions,
waiting for him to awaken from his nap.

"Did the wee people bring you a dream?" asked his mother,
holding him in her arms and smiling.
"Yes" replied the boy, "and the hermit did too."

With the boy safe and sound in his mother's lap,
I closed the book of my grandfather
and placed it again among the soft weavings of spiders,
by a window filled with light.

Down the steps went I from the attic
and back into the story of my own life
surrounded by robins in all of the trees

We All Return to Each Other

There is a soft tapping at my shoulder,
a hint of fingers urging me awake,
gathering me into the dreamy half-spirit world
where eyes can see into themselves
and floors drift underneath

An arm enfolds me, the embrace of my long-dead father
who wants to know that Mother is comfortable in her bed,
that the blue-framed pictures of their children still hang
overhead,
straight, in proper order, and have not been disturbed.

I feel the kindness of his presence,
his gaze falling on the sleeping form of his wife who,
huddled calmly under an afghan her own mother wove,
is breathing in long, unhurried breaths on this,
her last night.

He has come to be reassured, for peace of mind,
to know that I am doing for her what must be done
for a mother dying in her own bed,
keeping her warm and sitting by her feet, singing.

He nods approvingly,
removes his arm from mine,
and lifts away.

Argument

On the night we could not hear each other,
Our words like sharpened teeth, like traps,
you left for dinner, alone,
and I found a bed to lie down on,
looking up at the ceiling, for guidance, for a sign,
for anything that would tell me what to do,
what would come next,
trying hard to make sense, think logically,
now that the only thing that made sense
had broken into pieces,
and while I was waiting, an image of myself floated by,
descending the stairs,
taking the painting of my grandmother from the wall,
and the small photograph of my mother in her wedding gown
that was tucked in the china cabinet, next to her crystal,
and pictures of the kids when they were small,
and a few changes of clothes thrown into a suitcase,
putting all of these in the back of the truck,
and driving away in the dark,
leaving no note,
saying no good-bye,
not even patting the dog's head.

It seemed so sad to watch myself doing that,
to imagine you wondering forever where I'd gone,
that I got up off the bed and began cleaning the bathroom
which was where you found me when you arrived home.

Compass

(For all devoted older brothers everywhere,
and in particular, mine)

It is odd, you growing older,
as if the gods of younger brothers
should remain ageless and immortal,
as if time has nothing in common with you,
a different vocabulary, another language.

There is the image of the two of us,
first memory, unearthed consciousness,
silent in the darkened chamber of the boys' room.
Someone has extinguished the light
and the fixture above, a faded bowl
encircled by sailing ships,
is yet glowing,
we little knowing you would follow those ships
from Devon Island to Istanbul,
China to Barcelona,
the rain forests and glaciers to Afghanistan
while I, settled in the obscurity of the Ozarks,
receive postcards from you like the furious wake

of the long ago ships still circling the ceiling
on Beaconsfield Road.

You received me at five,
as a child would a gift,
hurtling out of your early years
like a rocket in its booster stage,
like a furious bantam
fighting your way to the beauty and mystery of the world,
like an inventor readying himself for inspection
of the materials at hand,
your refuge of plywood walls and doors below us
a cocoon, an embryo,
entrails of crystal radios glowing like silver veins and
capillaries,
dissections performed on prehistoric toasters,
Electrolux vacuums found missing from the closet above.

You learned the intricate physics
of how things worked
before launching yourself into the universe,
an artist, a mapmaker, a documentarian.

I want to imagine the two of us in our 80s,
wending our way once more toward the summit of Chicorua,
looking north across the vastness of the Presidentials
toward Maine and Canada,
wondering what brought us here, what tangle of paths,

what fluid puzzle of grandparents so long ago
leaving the shtetls of Lithuania and the Ukraine
to allow us this moment?

I want to ponder the power and luminosity of life
that I should stand next to you, my guide, my compass,
arms around each other, shoulders for each other to lean on,
knowing that as long as you are next to me,
I will be able to take another step.

Chava

Waiting for your lifetime to begin
Is a lifetime in itself
the light of your eyes
the wail of your voice
glow of your soul upon us
waiting for your lifetime to begin
watching shadows fade in fade out
wondering which is you which is me
wandering about snowy streets
peering in windows, fumbling for keys,
doing things people do on winter days

Isn't it mysterious this hold you have
on me
our eyes haven't even met

A Thought for the Next Century

My youngest child's voice rises
Above the hum of the radio,
I am making breakfast for him, served in bed.
"How many years will I live in the 21st century?"
"Sixty-five, I'd say, you've got a long way to go."
"How many will you?"
"Twenty-five, if I am lucky," I shout from the kitchen,
"If I keep my cholesterol down."
A pause, a silence, then:
"I don't think that is good," he offers, a hint of worry, of
concern.
"It will be sad living so long without you."

Welcome Home

Mary Ahern stood above the whitewashed wall
in Araglen, County Cork
(her son looking for all the world like a Kennedy)
and said "Welcome Home".

Home, I pondered,
Through introductions and a turf fire and sweetened Irish
whiskey.

Home, I am in the home of Kathleen's ancestors,
her people now my people,
our children with the blood of Celtic farmers
and Hebrew shepherds in their veins.

Did her grandfather John Crotty imagine
as he closed the gate to Araglen in 1910
and made the for the docks at Cobh
that he would be bringing me a gift?

And what of Morris Gouterman,
fleeing the czar's army in 1880,
did he dream of a grandson in Arkansas

on a beautiful October eve 108 years later,
vowing to love forever his sweet Irish princess?

It is chance, it is luck
At work in our lives,
Scripting episode after episode,
The real life video awash with drama,
Adventures launched like fragile vessels,
Bobbing upon the rime waves,
"tempest tossed" by God's turn of the dial.

Who can argue with chance
When its special effects
Are what you see around you,
Our forebears closing gates and boarding ships,
Making shoes and building cabinets
Having babies who turn into fathers and mothers
And finally us?

Who can argue with chance
When the credits outnumber the debits,
When the true meaning in all of this
Is grasped in the laughter of children
In the sweetness of a woman's love,
In the depths of the words: welcome home?

Ralph, 1947

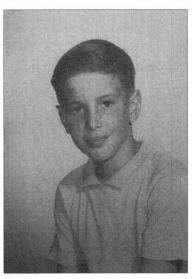

Ralph, 1950—3 years old

Ralph and Bob at Beverly Beach, 1950

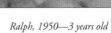

Ralph, 1957—10 years old

Ralph, 1970

Taken in 1973 in the Mokelumne wilderness area in the
Sierra Nevadas on a hiking trip with his brother

Hillary Clinton and Ralph, 1993

Ralph, 2017

Ben and Ralph, 1983

Ralph with his son Liam Nesson, and grandchildren Eleanor (9 months) and Chloe (4 years old)

Ralph and his brother, Bob Nesson, on a ridge above the Falling Waters trail in the New Hampshire White Mountains

Ralph and Kate Conway with their granddaughter, Chloe Nesson (6 years old)

Ralph with his grandchildren Jett Boyett (9 months) and Chloe Nesson (2 years old), 2014

From left to right: Kenny Boyett, Tate Boyett, Kate Conway, Ralph Nesson, Chloe Nesson, Liam Nesson, Molly Munro, Anjie Jae, Ben Nesson, Chava Boyett, Jett Boyett, Jessica Andrews, Eleanor Nesson. Santa Cruz, California, 2014

Ralph in Yachats, Oregon, 2010

Ralph singing his favorite song "Stormy Monday," 2013

Ralph, 2019

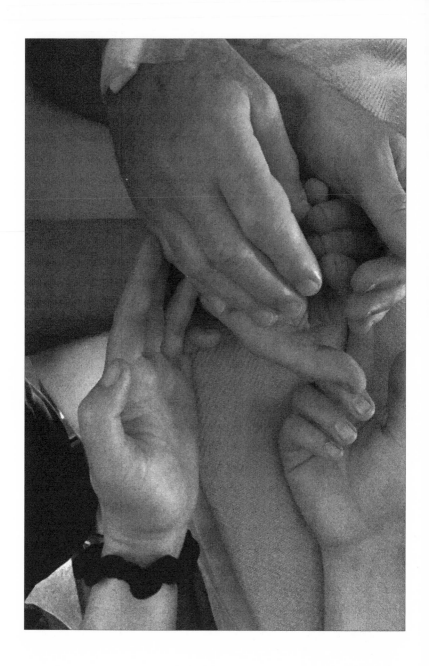

PLACE

Vineyard

Went there as a child, didn't see
that strange half light of another era
of mackinacks
of indian faces
arbor ways fronting old frame houses
grandfathers closing in the chickens
willows brushing rough stone walls
church steeple looking out to sea

Half Moon Bay

In a lump at the bar
gordon warms himself with revelations
shoulders turned in, nose down
tongue dangling toward his beer
"someone give 'em a cup of coffee"
from an old man to the left
gordon's head jerks up
body sways toward the voice
"I'm in my element
And intend to remain so"

Regalo De Dios

(When Spanish babies are born with no acknowledged
father, "gift from god" is written on the birth
certificate where the father's name belongs)

Ache of new life
in the act of becoming,
breath of new life
in the spume of arriving,
heart of new life,
in the fury of stirring,
soul of new life,
in the tranquility of being.

Receiving you in our midst
with the certainty that you are with us
as the sun and moon are with us,
as the earth and the ocean are with us,
as our ancestors are with us,
as God, who is with us,
places miracles in our arms.

Fenway

This is the same Fenway Park
Where I was brought at the age of four
To blink at the green brilliance of the outfield grass
And inhale deeply of roasted peanuts
And cherry blend
Without understanding the game at all.

The same Fenway Park where I sat in general admission
grandstand
Watching Jimmy Piersall turn his back to home plate
And panic by the flagpole, waving his arms and howling like a
dog at the moon
Only to be guided to the dugout and McLean's Hospital
By men in white coats.

The same Fenway Park
Where Ted Williams homered in his last at bat
And called it quits,
Jim Wallen and I standing in awe of the Splendid Splinter
When he, at last, tipped his hat
To acknowledge there were fans out there
Paying his way into the Hall of Fame.

This is the same Fenway Park
Where my sons, raised so far away
Pray at the shrine of my childhood
Inhale peanut smells
Long for hot dogs and mustard
And wonder if they can get around on Roger Clemens'
fastball.

To a Collapsing Barn

Grayfaced and buckling,
pulled by unforgiving time out of plumb,
swaying and creaking toward earth
with each breath of wind,
an epitaph for those
who lifted heart and hand to build you,
a sign to those who failed,
to keep you whole.
A cemetery nearby holds the bones of craftsmen,
who framed your rafters,
who laid your center pole in place,
and wove your joints as from a loom,
who rested once the last plank was fitted,
ate the Lord's reward on checkered tablecloths,
and gazed upon your sturdiness, your form.

As winter claws at your seams,
the scorch of summer's breath pushes out your nails,
and the relentless tug of earth is given into,
there will be a call to you to rest,
swaying and falling back to earth,
sending up a giant cloud of dust,

the sound of something ending,
the muted letting go of what you were.

A Train to Ronda

We are being carried high into the Serrania,
Kestrels and martins flying past the windows like paper
planes
A party of young English and Americans ahead of me
And well-dressed Granadans all around.

I will not know until later,
After I have written my account and given it to Brigit
That Juaquin has never been to Ronda
And his wife will tell him about my discoveries
And they will leave his relations in Malaga
To drive the route through the mountains
To arrive at the parador overlooking the gorge
From which the Falange henchmen of his father
Pushed the Republican fighters to their deaths.

But now, I am listening to the young English speakers,
Their laughter interspersed with obscenities,
Harsh corners of words cutting angles through their smoke.
This will be strange to the Granadans,
A vulgar pantomime, a poor harvest of cacophonies,
Nothing pleasing to the ear to begin with
And less will they know what to do with words in bad taste.

Or so I think, being used to recoiling.
It becomes important to feign incomprehension,
Keeping my eyes averted and aloof,
Looking out toward the apparitions of white villages
Relieved, I leave the train in search of shelter for the night.
It is raining and I have yet to see the gorge.

Brubeck, 1996

The fingers remain long and tapered,
known for their sense of direction on the keyboard,
a certainty to where they land,
as if by floating gently, quickly down and up and down again,
they can rearrange the melodics,
the flow of any syncopation coming through.

When he was younger and I was thirteen,
there were marble columns surrounding us,
operatic boxes, the echo of fugues and adagios,
the hint of something larger than jazz,
as if his music were not grand enough,
as if he might have wandered across the wrong stage,
a symphony saboteur bent on bringing with him
the buzz of honky-tonks and carnivals,
of every blue Monday midnight lounge on the deep south side
or Mass Avenue and Washington Street dives,
their lights hushed and muted, shoulders of patrons hunched,
smokin' and drinkin' into the wee hours while the musicians
wail and moan,
staccato riffs pouring from the keys, the skins and horns and
bass,
as if he might have had the high brows stripping off their ties,

smiling knowingly to each other, eyes half closed, fingers tapping,
swaying back and forth to something in their bones.

His back is bowed now
from years of laying down versions of Take Five,
he is moving across the stage tentatively,
a hand at his elbow to help him to the bench,
Joe Morello gone,
Paul Desmond gone,
and he an old man with fingers
still rearranging the mathematics,
still moving up and down the keyboard,
the fever as sweet and strong as ever.

Among the Trees

If it is about the trees that we are here
It must also be about us and who we are

If it is about the finite and fragile beauty of the earth that we
are here,
It must be about the lives we lead and how we live them

And if it is about what grows and should be left to grow
Then it is about us and what we know
To be true about ourselves and why we come to be here
And what there is of value
To be preserved

If it is about a sense of responsibility
To the earth, to the trees, to all live things
And how we either steward them or not

That is either yes or no

And, if it is no, if that is the sad choice we make in mockery,
in blindness to the miracles around us
We are destined to awaken each morning and find less and
less of who we are

And less of what we are
And awaken each morning to less around us except
What makes little sense and carries with it few hints of beauty,
Nothing left to preserve or remember,
Only a thick and fragrant shadow of what once was.

And, if yes, let us all awaken among the trees
and find the will to sing like doves
and find the will to raise our arms like winds
and make of life a sacred trust
an inheritance,
a prayer to all that has been given to us,
let us not forsake it,

If it is about the trees that we are here,
It must be every one of us, among the trees.

Two Photographs

Emboldened by the flash
her face illuminates
the dark silhouettes behind,
uncles with their beer and hats.

There is a holiness about her,
and a petulance as well,
juxtapositions that oddly work.

I place her next to a flower,
the red stamen of the hibiscus
enshrined by soft mollusked leaves,
a hint of perfection, slight and implied,
dispassionate,
as if annoyed by the camera interrupting its life.

Stamp Night

It is the dark and murky heat of south Florida
Which gives rise to this,
The confluence of replica Italianate design
And fascination with all things Disney,
A sparsely furnished mansion,
Floor of vinyl imitation oak begging for carpeting,
Oil paintings of babes in Fantasia,
And Cinderella's pumpkin coach
Displayed upon the walls,
Aesthetic path to the dining room,
Where the work of stamp night will be done.

Stacks of envelopes and pre-sorted letters
Await the family circle,
On a table at this hour,
Where dinner might be served.
But now they gather with other appetites,
Grandparents and parents and aunts and uncles
Called by the lawyer couple every Monday
To stuff and seal the envelopes
And apply the bulk rate stamp
For forwarding to drivers under the influence,
Attorneys' services available,

The best possible deal under the circumstances
At a very reasonable rate.

Drivers of every extraction,
Haitians, Chinese, Cubans, Portugese
Along with the local country boys,
Who drank too much and got pulled over,
Or got pulled *out* if they hit something,
All needing a way to stay on the road or out of jail.
Convenient payment schedule, reads the letter,
Or anything of value convertible to cash.
And the best deal possible in court,
These lawyers know what they are doing,
They specialize.

After the letters are readied for mailing,
A cup of coffee, a sweet dessert,
Some gossip about the family,
How the bachelor uncle can't hold his temper,
Or the cousin who went bankrupt but kept his fancy car,
They will sit and talk until the old ones are ready
And someone will drive them home,
No one will care what was said or quite remember,
And the stories will be repeated the next week,
The laughs coming a little harder each time.

On another night,
All the judges and district attorneys and arresting cops for

miles around

Will receive invitations to a fine catered dinner at the lawyer couple's house,

And they won't have to lick stamps or stuff envelopes like the family does,

It will be a relaxing evening together,

People of the same class

Just getting to know each other a little better,

Out of school, informally, you understand.

Requiem for Rwanda

Acts beyond words,
Beyond explanation or description,
Beyond futility,
A challenge to our capacity to believe,
We are capable of this.

Erosion of faith,
Expulsion from the very core
Of what it means to breathe life into each other.

Innocence defiled,
Imploded,
On our scraped and bleeding knees for reprieve,
It never comes, never comes.

Falling further and further into the charnel house,
From what we ever thought possible,
Finding nothing to grasp onto,
Nothing.

Acts beyond words, hurling the holocaust at us
Until we are all pariahs,

God has had enough of us,
We are not worthy.

And yet, even still,
A voice remains in prayer,
The voice of a small child entreats:
If there is somewhere I can be safe,
Show it to me, I want to see it,
I want to be there now,
If there is a glimmer, a sliver of hope,
A possibility of having a life,
If there is a life,
I choose it now.

Backyard Haikus, Almost

New day streaked with rust,
has been here before,
maybe?

Mockingbird hostility,
blue jay indifference,
she's hungry.

Woodpecker shrieks jungle call,
ignores seed,
eats feeder post instead.

Bleached bones of dog,
dry under porch,
avoiding sun, no barking.

Neighbor gone, died last year,
his son religiously
still mowing lawn.

Old grille,
rusted through,
awaits next instructions.

Catalpa tree
drops long spiny seed,
ignores me.

Cracked earth,
awaiting rain,
breathes like moon.

Green snake,
garden hermit,
won't show this year.

Tomato plant,
Like old man,
tangled with weeds.

I'll either rake today,
or read a book,
it doesn't matter.

FRIENDS AND NEIGHBORS

Free at Last

She was often there,
ascending South College Avenue,
her violin case like luggage
packed with folded music captive,
claiming its freedom on the square.

Her son Isaac would be slightly ahead,
scouting the territory on his bicycle,
an understudy in the ways of her world.

To offer them a ride
was to interrupt their rhythm,
their determination
to slow down the pace of things.

I would bring her newspapers in winter,
stacking the day's headlines
on the front porch.
She would roll them into logs for warmth,
throwing taxes, wars, speeches,
and weather reports into her wood-burning stove.
Eventually there was too much journalism in brown paper
sacks,

and I would know to stop,
the temperature inside oversubscribed.

Later, when she was sick,
her face narrowed and gaunt,
she grasped my hand and apologized.
"It's nothing sexual" she said among tubes and catheters
and businesslike nurses.
"I only want to feel your strength,
I don't feel very strong today."

And now she is gone entirely,
taking an era in this town with her.
If ever I wonder how much I have lost to conformity,
to doing what is expected,
and ignoring what is truest within me,
I will think of her
playing music to the flowers,
knowing that they heard.

McNeil Cabin, Larue

The professors were in China, or France,
Touring along the Rhine,
Or climbing an Alaskan glacier,
While you and I sat in their cabin in Larue,
Peering out at the mist,
Rain tapping on the roof,
Maps of their travels papering the walls,
Scribbled notations bemoaning the fact
That the trains were slow or not at all in Prague,
That this road or that was bordered with wildflowers,
That the grapes in Bordeaux were unlike any they had ever
tasted.

Now the professors
Require assisted living,
She almost unable to see,
He unable to remember,
And the maps in the cabin
Are yellow and crumbling.

The Neighbor, I

He never approved
Of my father's style of discipline
And saw in my brother
Much more than an angry kid.

He never approved of my father, period
Who'd avoided the Second World War
And had no words for him
Beyond the obligatory nod.

Whenever he had the chance,
He'd ask my brother what he was tinkering with,
And would tell him how he, too,
Had taken things apart to see how they worked.

When a war came for me,
He limped over and told me it was my duty to enlist.
"Your old man was yellow but you needn't be."

Perhaps he confused me with my brother
Who'd paratrooped in the South and whooped and screamed
"Geronimo"
While jumping out of planes.

I looked him in the eye,
Told him it was a bad war,
That I wanted no part of killing babies.
With a disgusted look, he turned and went back next door,
Yelling over his shoulder:
"No such thing as a bad war
When your country tells you to go."

The Neighbor, II

He had no use for my father
Who'd avoided the Second World War
While he, with a permanent limp,
Kept his war stories to himself.

He had only contempt
For my father's style of discipline,
And saw in my brother
Much more than an angry kid.

Whenever he had the chance,
He'd ask my brother what he was tinkering with,
Telling him how he too
Had taken things apart to see how they worked.

When a war came for me,
He told me it was my duty to enlist,
Your old man was yellow
But you don't need to be.

Perhaps he confused me with my brother
Who'd paratrooped in the South,

Whooping and screaming Geronimo
As he leapt out of planes.

I told him it was a bad war
And that I wanted no part in killing babies
Or following generals
Who'd make a mistake.

No such thing as a bad war, he snarled
When the flag is at stake,
Words thrown over his shoulder
As he limped back next door.

Old Friends

We were sitting together,
The four of us
Who had put on our first baseball gloves together
And gone to each others' Bar Mitzvahs,
Dressed like little gentlemen,
And kissed the same girls
While early 1960s music
Played on scratchy hi-fis.

Who had sat in the same musty classrooms
Year after year
And watched each other put on height and weight
And finally gone our own ways,
Expecting to see each other, as usual.

We were sitting together,
The four of us
Thirty years later,
Good dinner, effortless talk,
When I went to pay the bill.

A hand reached out to stop me,

"We'll take care of it", one said,
"Rich doctors can afford it."

I pushed the hand away
And handed the waiter my check.

"I'm the one who invited you," I replied,
"And I'm the one who'll pay."

Of Leaving

(For Lisa Martinovic)

Each time one of us is gone
And it is the act of disappearing that matters most,
I get that abandoned feeling,
The sense of being left upon an abstract rock,
Surrounded by dark mist, lost to myself,
Invisible to others,
As if my birth had not occurred,
An unexposed spirit
Seeking a path to the light.

I wonder where we go,
All of us,
Where do we end up out of sight?

. . . Meditating in a cabin in the forest,
Hard, flattened dirt for floor, no running water,
Halfway up the side of a mountain,
Only a cat for company?

. . . On Folsom Street, feeding strays and drinking
Thunderbird,

Waiting for the sun's arrival,
Only to fall asleep on a bench by the wading pool,
Nudged awake by cops doing their duty,
Trudging over to the coffee and biscuit line at St. Theresa's
Church,
Been there every day for a week.

. . . Working in a second cousin's credit office,
Dunning people who say they are someone else,
Yanking on a lonely mother with two kids
Who hasn't made her payments on the refrigerator loan.

Or, like Lisa, answering the far-off siren of the fame goddess,
Seeking holy poetic enlightenment in haunted North Beach
dives,
Memorizing lines and praying to be noticed,
Ripping open souls, revealing the oozing contents within,
Frantically delaying all gratification in gasps,
Writing down what we remember happened to us,
Yes or no for a purpose,
Perhaps to be revealed at a later date?

Each time one of us leaves,
There is a void begging to be filled by the next arrival,
Illuminated by phantoms bathed in verse and collective myth,
The dregs of humanity marching along the parade route,
Saints and angels all working their way through madness and
sanity and back,

Inspecting this sad life and entering it in full bloom,
Inhabiting this sanctuary for seconds and eons,
Paralyzed with fear, connected by endless dreams,
Flaunting the pain, writhing in the throes of relentless passion,
Digging deep in the search for meaning,
Flying high on the kundalini of ecstatic experience,
Rubbing our dripping, seething genitalia in a furious rush to lubricated nirvana,
Asking for nothing but accepting all,
Burning iridescently burning inside our skin for centuries,
Burning fiercely with the fueled incendiaries of life in the extreme,
Until,
All organic content sizzled and roasted and fried beyond recognition,

We ascend through the clouds towards distant heaven,
Blessed and sacred memories for those left behind.

Each time one of us leaves,
The earth moans, the coyotes let out with ferocious howling,
Gnashing their teeth, praying for another chance,
Reluctantly whispering goodbye.

Charlie's Barbershop

Rained-on men like parentheses
Punctuate Charlie's,
Flooding the plastic green backed chairs,
Advancing theories about the railroad,
While puddles drown their feet.

There was a collision today,
Another customer for St. Mary's and the wrecker.

The rained-on men debate railroad sovereignty:
This town owes its soul to the Missouri Pacific,
It was here before Mrs. Howie's pecan trees,
Before her father's foundry
And before Number 7 turned into El Paso Street.
Get hit by a diesel and it's your own damned fault.
The railroad was here first.

Trimming the hair of a ten year old,
Old Charlie smiles and thinks of the apples
Up on Crow mountain as the engines homestead
One street over.

Ablaze

(For Ginny and Nick Masullo)

It is there in the way you look at each other,
a knowing glance, the lowering of an eyelid,
the tenderness of a smile, of a good-bye.

There in holding the hand of your child,
if only for a moment, if only to reassure,
in the way your plans are made,
on the water,
on the ice,
on bicycles,
in the visits to parents,
walks through distant villages
filled with the mystery of your past.

During separate moments,
When one is writing poetry
and the other easing through chord progressions,
the sound of music and images lilting in the air.

During the hard times
when the needs of others

push your own needs aside,
and you give each other what you need
to ease on through.

During changes which inevitably come,
sighing and shifting and lifting into each phase of the moon,
the gentle aging of myths
with which you and we are all surrounded.

It is there for the rest of us to witness in the touch of a hand,
the knowing and seeking and reaching toward each other,
the comfort of arms entwined, hearts beating together,
so mutually and earnestly and soundly together
allowing space, inhalation of breath,
awareness what each other needs,
the giving of it instinctively

It is all there, in bloom, in full flower,
in one and the other,
a passion enduring,
the flame yet kindled, the fire ablaze.

Birch

I wanted to tell this boy,
this boy with whom I take walks with our dog in America,
all about Spain,
About how my high school teacher would describe her
country to us,
the click of flamenco heels and castanets,
the mysteries of the Alhambra,
the molluscan taste of paella,
the desolate hills of La Mancha,
the orange trees of Sevilla,
the Spain so much more than conjugating verbs
or learning to trill.

How I waited forty years to go there
and when finally I did,
it felt like coming home,
How Don Paco took us in,
and Dori and Antonio showed us their land in the campo,
and how the waitress Mariana laughed when I used the wrong
word to order olives.

How the narrow streets of Cordoba were home,
the mosques and alcazabas,

the little bakery where the owner wore black
and sadly sold baguettes
and wept for her mother, lying dead in the cemetery the past
25 years,
her shop was home too,
as was the bus which always stopped at the Venta del Pobre,
So the driver could have his cigarette and coffee
before continuing on to Algeria,
All the passengers waiting patiently and smoking,
though it wasn't allowed.

I wanted to tell the boy about the country I saw
that I remember and long for in the dark,
but his mind was on other things,
it was he who had stories to tell,
designs in his head of submersibles and mechanical
amphibians,
helicopters which could crawl under water,
then fly above the sea,
launch pads and cranes and every variety of rocket booster
assembly,
toys like the embryonic creations
of a born engineer.

I would save Spain for another year.

A Small Cantina in the Old City of San Juan

There is a photograph of Amelia on the wall by the dessert
case,
She is thirty years younger and wearing a tennis outfit,
grass courts are behind her, a wood racquet is in her hands,
she is smiling, her dark hair long and wavy, palm trees are all
around
and we come to know that the greats like Pancho Gonzalez
and Anna Perez and others whose names she cannot recall
thought she had great potential, gave her lessons, and encour-
aged her to compete.

But her knee developed problems that only got worse,
a botched operation gave her a permanent limp,
arthritis set in and a tennis career was only a dream of the
past,
replaced by bad marriages and ingrates for children,
losing nice homes in divorce proceedings, paying good
money to bad lawyers,
coming here to the old city to make a new start.

She is now heavy set, smoking cigarettes, still limping,
yelling at her helper who can't seem to do anything right

and receives blame for dust in the window, bathrooms that
are not clean,
overcooked beans, and water glasses not brought to the
customers.
The woman is followed wherever she goes, cannot get Amelia
off her back,
yells at her in Spanish that *she* is the one who is lazy
throws her apron onto the counter and storms out the door.

"She will be back in an hour, this happens all the time
when her husband is drinking, don't pay her any mind," says
Amelia, "Now what would you like to order?"

Made in the USA
Coppell, TX
27 June 2021